BLACK PANTHER

A NATION UNDER OUR FEET: PART 3

MARVEL

ABDO
Spotlight

ABDOBOOKS.COM

Reinforced library bound edition published in 2020 by Spotlight,
a division of ABDO, PO Box 398166, Minneapolis, Minnesota 55439.
Spotlight produces high-quality reinforced library bound editions for
schools and libraries. Published by agreement with Marvel Characters, Inc.

Printed in the United States of America, North Mankato, Minnesota.
042019
092019

THIS BOOK CONTAINS RECYCLED MATERIALS

Library of Congress Control Number: 2018965952

Publisher's Cataloging-in-Publication Data

Names: Coates, Ta-Nehisi, author. | Stelfreeze, Brian; Martin, Laura; Sprouse, Chris; Story, Karl, illustrators.
Title: A nation under our feet / writer: Ta-Nehisi Coates; art: Brian Stelfreeze ; Laura Martin ; Chris Sprouse ; Karl Story.
Description: Minneapolis, Minnesota : Spotlight, 2020 | Series: Black Panther
Summary: With a dramatic upheaval in Wakanda on the horizon, T'Challa knows his kingdom needs to change to survive, but he struggles to find balance in his roles as king and the Black Panther.
Identifiers: ISBN 9781532143519 (pt. 1 ; lib. bdg.) | ISBN 9781532143526 (pt. 2 ; lib. bdg.) | ISBN 9781532143533 (pt. 3 ; lib. bdg.) | ISBN 9781532143540 (pt. 4 ; lib. bdg.) | ISBN 9781532143557 (pt. 5 ; lib. bdg.) | ISBN 9781532143564 (pt. 6 ; lib. bdg.)
Subjects: LCSH: Black Panther (Fictitious character)--Juvenile fiction. | Superheroes--Juvenile fiction. | Kings and rulers--Juvenile fiction. | Graphic novels--Juvenile fiction. | T'Challa, of Wakanda (Fictitious character)--Juvenile fiction.
Classification: DDC 741.5--dc23

ABDO
Spotlight

A Division of ABDO
abdobooks.com

BLACK PANTHER

AYO AND ANEKA -- FORMERLY OF THE DORA MILAJE, NOW KNOWN AS THE MIDNIGHT ANGELS -- ARE LIBERATING OPPRESSED WAKANDANS THAT THE CROWN HAS NEGLECTED FOR TOO LONG.

MEANWHILE, T'CHALLA TRACKED DOWN ZENZI, THE WOMAN WHO INCITED A RIOT AT THE GREAT MOUND, BUT FELL PREY TO HER MENTAL POWERS. DISTRACTING T'CHALLA WITH HIS GUILT OVER HIS SISTER SHURI'S DEATH, ZENZI ESCAPED.

EXCEPT SHURI HAD NOT TRULY DIED. HER SPIRIT NOW TRAVELS THE DJALIA, THE PLANE OF WAKANDAN MEMORY...

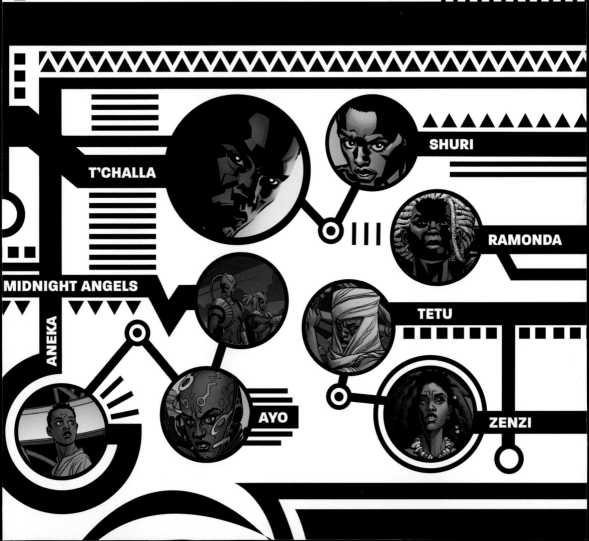

T'CHALLA

SHURI

RAMONDA

MIDNIGHT ANGELS

ANEKA

TETU

AYO

ZENZI

A NATION
UNDER OUR FEET

part **3**

writer **TA-NEHISI COATES**
artist **BRIAN STELFREEZE**
color artist **LAURA MARTIN**

letterer **VC's JOE SABINO**
design **MANNY MEDEROS**
logo **RIAN HUGHES**
cover by **BRIAN STELFREEZE**
and LAURA MARTIN
variant covers by
KYLE BAKER
SANFORD GREENE
assistant editor **CHRIS ROBINSON**
editor **WIL MOSS**
executive editor **TOM BREVOORT**

editor in chief **AXEL ALONSO**   chief creative officer **JOE QUESADA**
publisher **DAN BUCKLEY**   executive producer **ALAN FINE**

BLACK PANTHER created by
STAN LEE &
JACK KIRBY

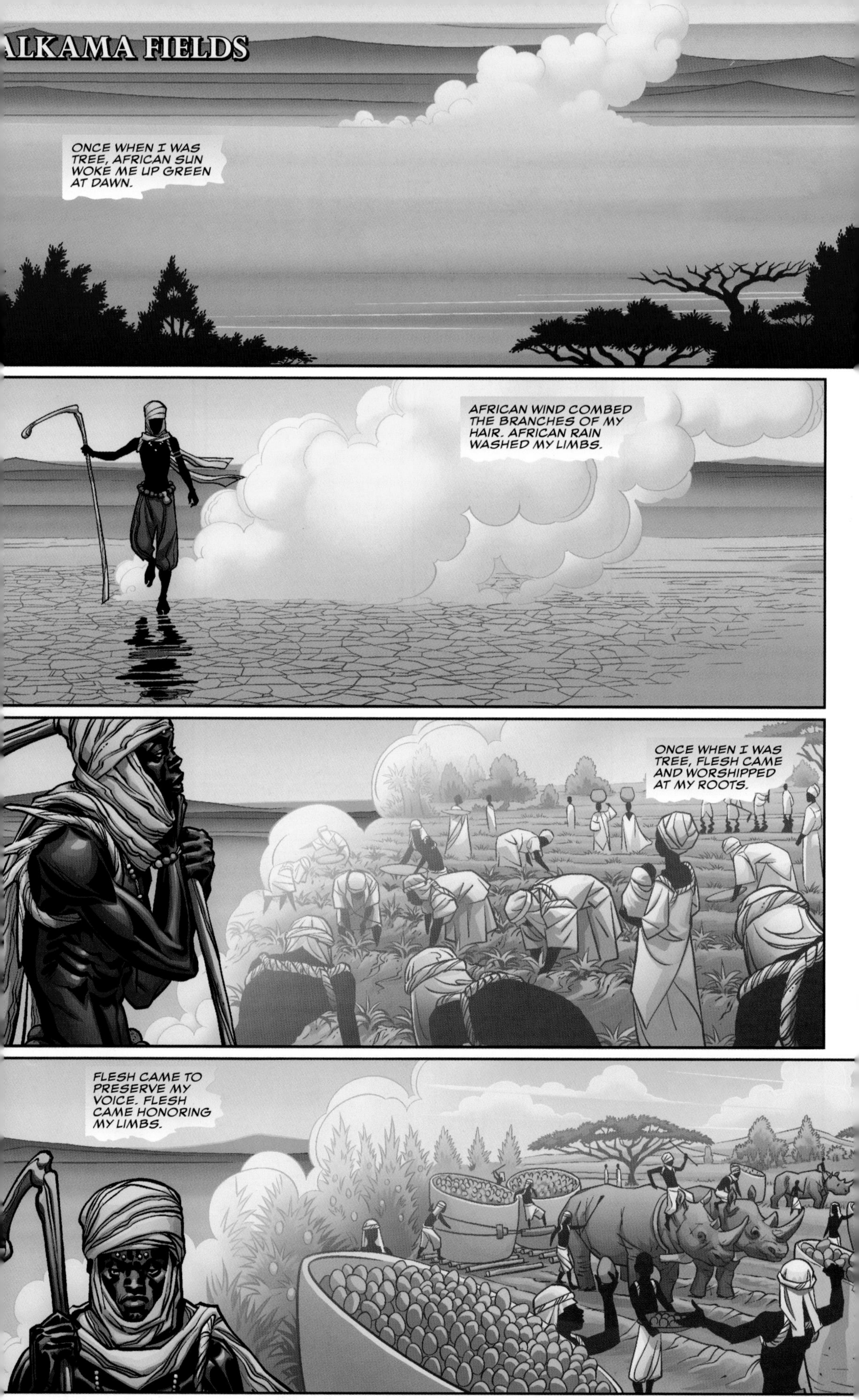
ALKAMA FIELDS
ONCE WHEN I WAS TREE, AFRICAN SUN WOKE ME UP GREEN AT DAWN.
AFRICAN WIND COMBED THE BRANCHES OF MY HAIR. AFRICAN RAIN WASHED MY LIMBS.
ONCE WHEN I WAS TREE, FLESH CAME AND WORSHIPPED AT MY ROOTS.
FLESH CAME TO PRESERVE MY VOICE. FLESH CAME HONORING MY LIMBS.

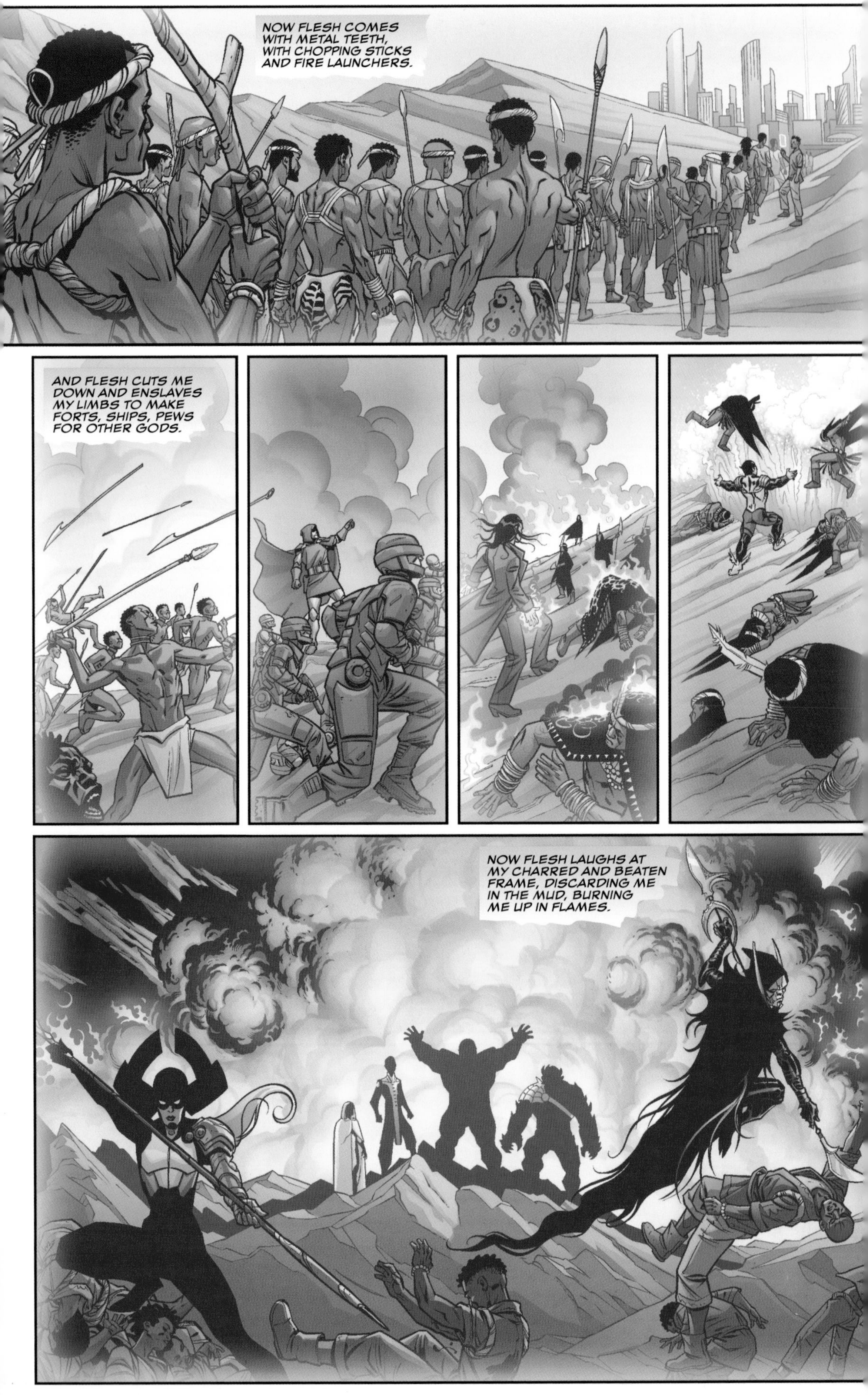
NOW FLESH COMES WITH METAL TEETH, WITH CHOPPING STICKS AND FIRE LAUNCHERS.
AND FLESH CUTS ME DOWN AND ENSLAVES MY LIMBS TO MAKE FORTS, SHIPS, PEWS FOR OTHER GODS.
NOW FLESH LAUGHS AT MY CHARRED AND BEATEN FRAME, DISCARDING ME IN THE MUD, BURNING ME UP IN FLAMES.

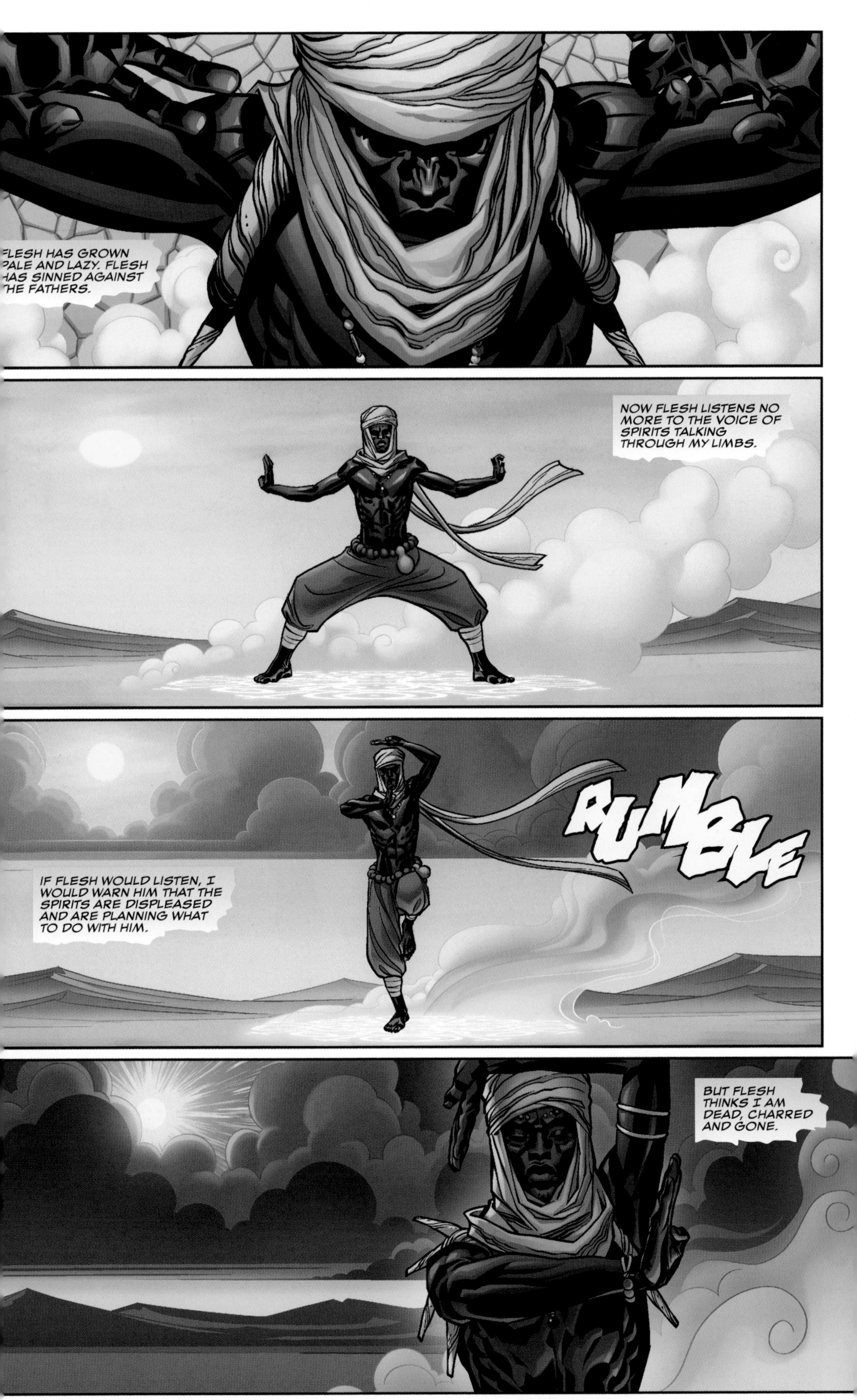
FLESH HAS GROWN PALE AND LAZY. FLESH HAS SINNED AGAINST THE FATHERS.
NOW FLESH LISTENS NO MORE TO THE VOICE OF SPIRITS TALKING THROUGH MY LIMBS.
RUMBLE
IF FLESH WOULD LISTEN, I WOULD WARN HIM THAT THE SPIRITS ARE DISPLEASED AND ARE PLANNING WHAT TO DO WITH HIM.
BUT FLESH THINKS I AM DEAD, CHARRED AND GONE.

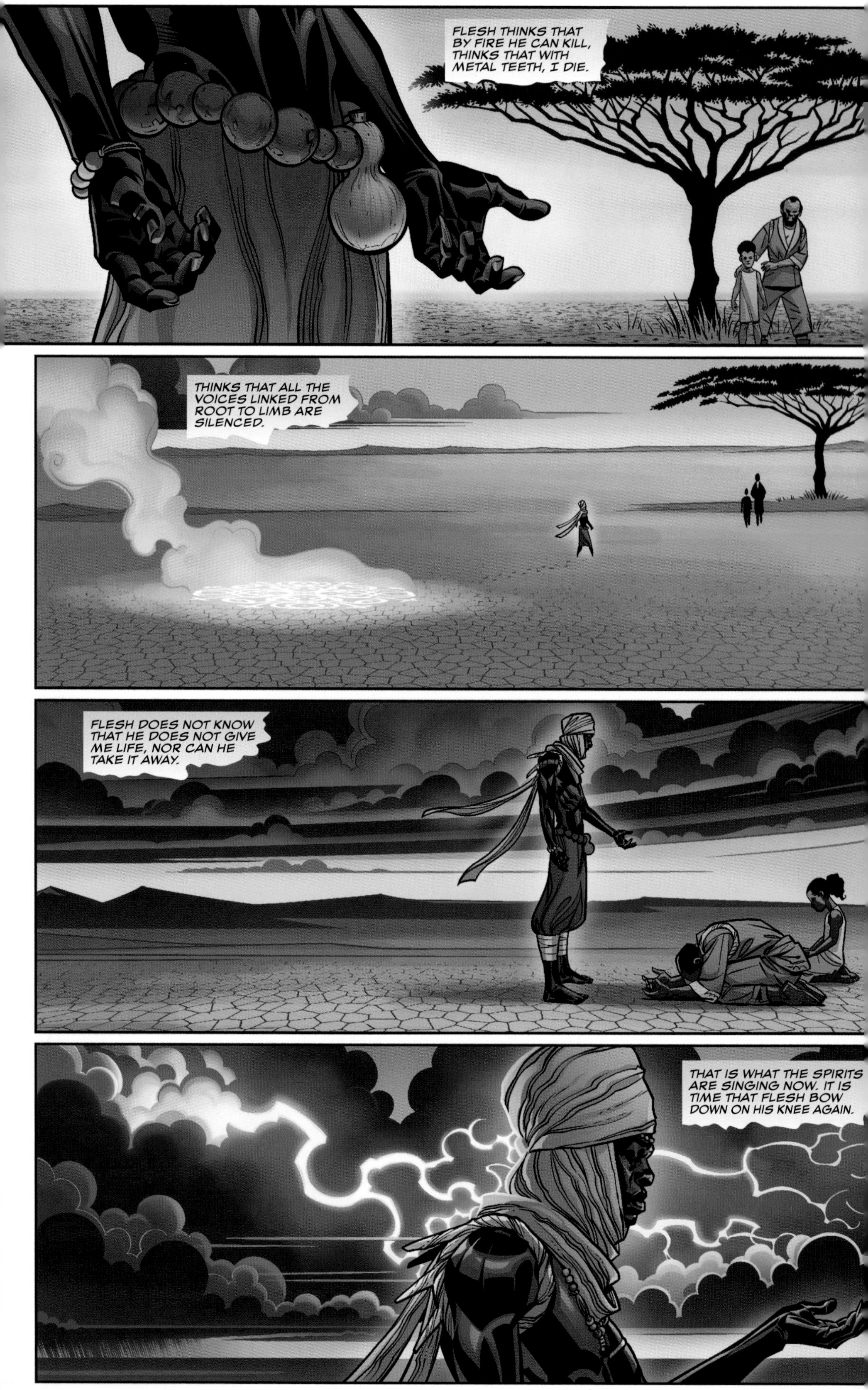
FLESH THINKS THAT BY FIRE HE CAN KILL, THINKS THAT WITH METAL TEETH, I DIE.
THINKS THAT ALL THE VOICES LINKED FROM ROOT TO LIMB ARE SILENCED.
FLESH DOES NOT KNOW THAT HE DOES NOT GIVE ME LIFE, NOR CAN HE TAKE IT AWAY.
THAT IS WHAT THE SPIRITS ARE SINGING NOW. IT IS TIME THAT FLESH BOW DOWN ON HIS KNEE AGAIN.

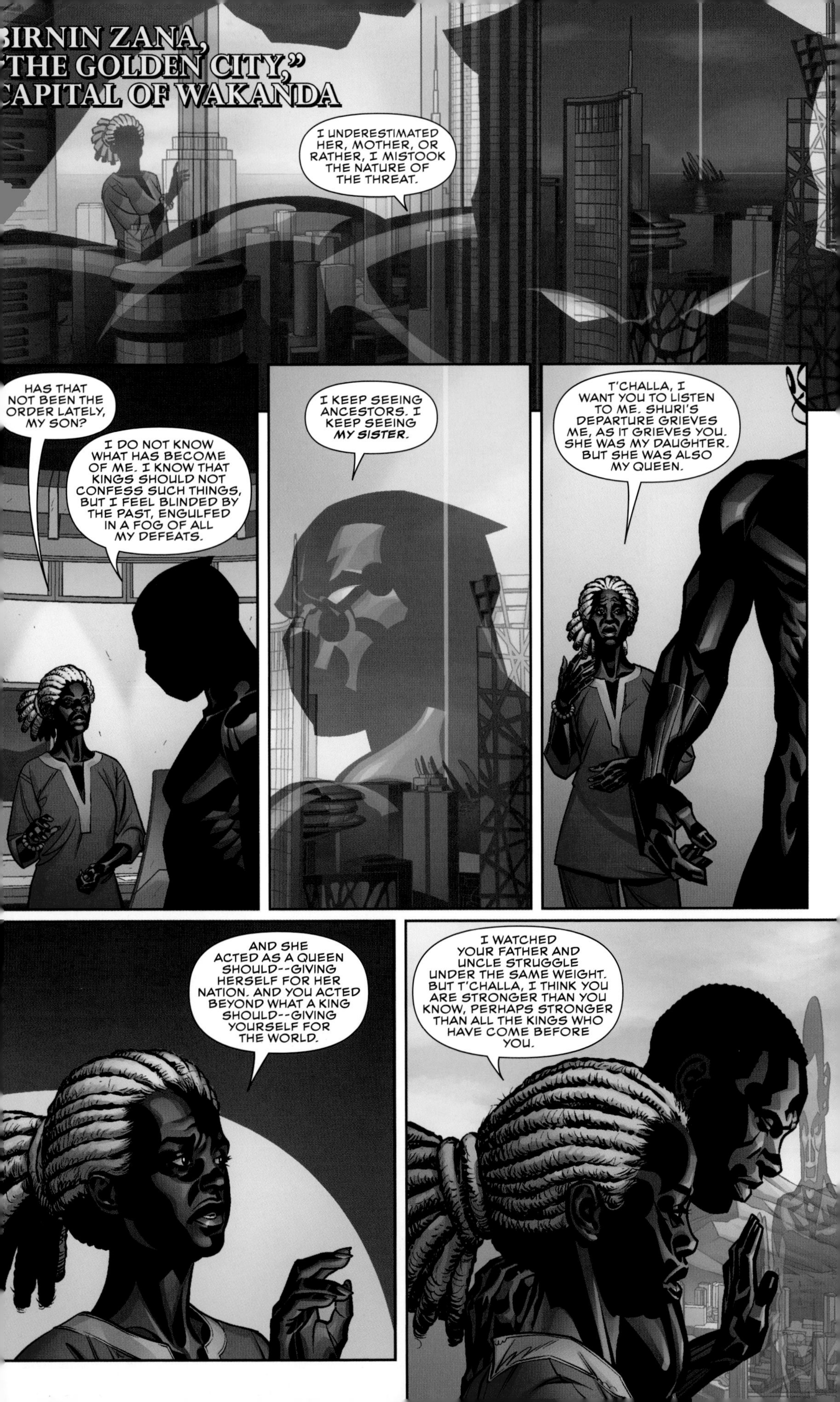
BIRNIN ZANA, "THE GOLDEN CITY," CAPITAL OF WAKANDA
I UNDERESTIMATED HER, MOTHER, OR RATHER, I MISTOOK THE NATURE OF THE THREAT.
HAS THAT NOT BEEN THE ORDER LATELY, MY SON?
I DO NOT KNOW WHAT HAS BECOME OF ME. I KNOW THAT KINGS SHOULD NOT CONFESS SUCH THINGS, BUT I FEEL BLINDED BY THE PAST, ENGULFED IN A FOG OF ALL MY DEFEATS.
I KEEP SEEING ANCESTORS. I KEEP SEEING *MY SISTER*.
T'CHALLA, I WANT YOU TO LISTEN TO ME. SHURI'S DEPARTURE GRIEVES ME, AS IT GRIEVES YOU. SHE WAS MY DAUGHTER. BUT SHE WAS ALSO MY QUEEN.
AND SHE ACTED AS A QUEEN SHOULD--GIVING HERSELF FOR HER NATION. AND YOU ACTED BEYOND WHAT A KING SHOULD--GIVING YOURSELF FOR THE WORLD.
I WATCHED YOUR FATHER AND UNCLE STRUGGLE UNDER THE SAME WEIGHT. BUT T'CHALLA, I THINK YOU ARE STRONGER THAN YOU KNOW, PERHAPS STRONGER THAN ALL THE KINGS WHO HAVE COME BEFORE YOU.

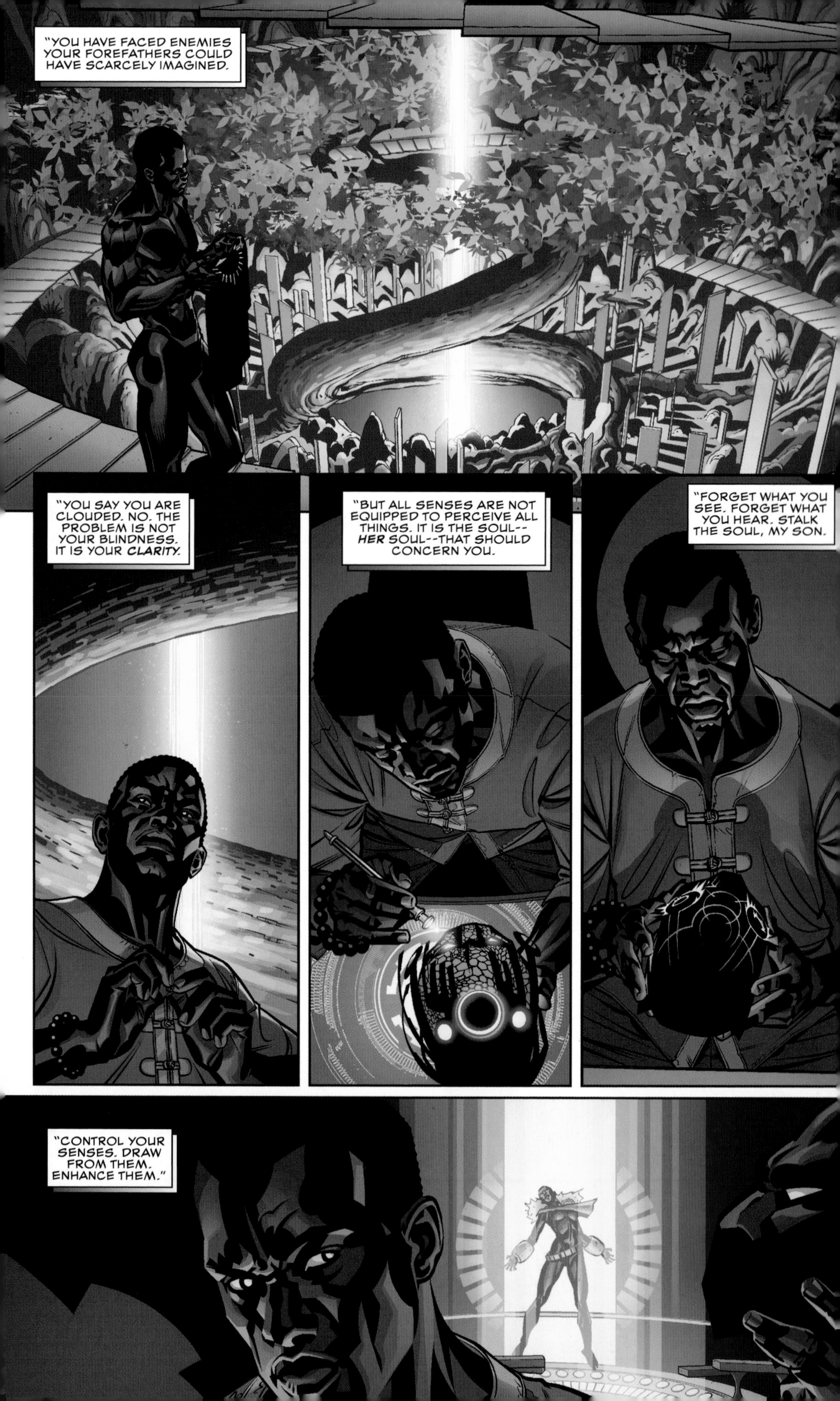
"YOU HAVE FACED ENEMIES YOUR FOREFATHERS COULD HAVE SCARCELY IMAGINED.
"YOU SAY YOU ARE CLOUDED. NO. THE PROBLEM IS NOT YOUR BLINDNESS. IT IS YOUR *CLARITY*.
"BUT ALL SENSES ARE NOT EQUIPPED TO PERCEIVE ALL THINGS. IT IS THE SOUL-- *HER* SOUL--THAT SHOULD CONCERN YOU.
"FORGET WHAT YOU SEE. FORGET WHAT YOU HEAR. STALK THE SOUL, MY SON.
"CONTROL YOUR SENSES. DRAW FROM THEM. ENHANCE THEM."

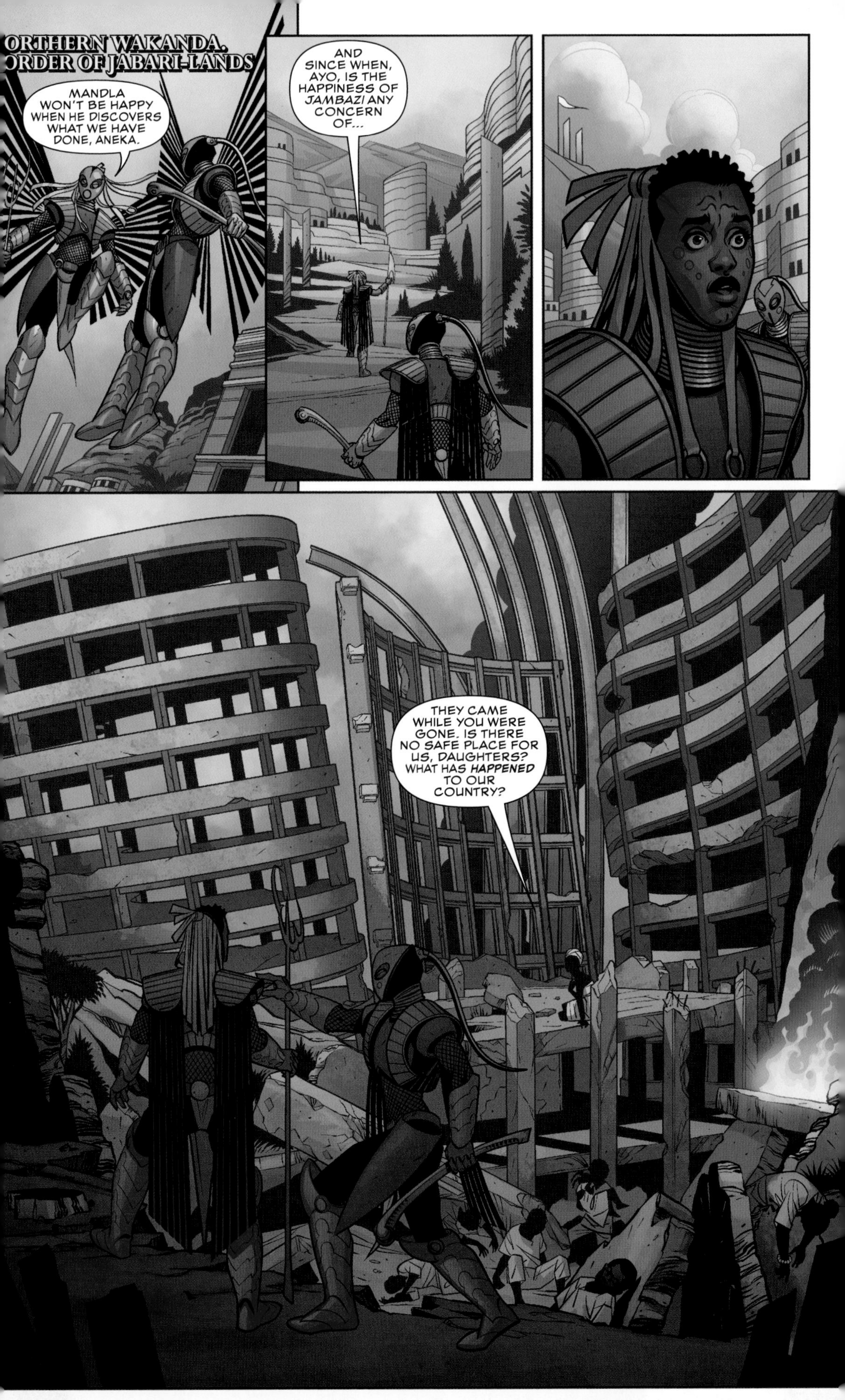

ORTHERN WAKANDA. ORDER OF JABARI-LANDS
MANDLA WON'T BE HAPPY WHEN HE DISCOVERS WHAT WE HAVE DONE, ANEKA.
AND SINCE WHEN, AYO, IS THE HAPPINESS OF JAMBAZI ANY CONCERN OF...
THEY CAME WHILE YOU WERE GONE. IS THERE NO SAFE PLACE FOR US, DAUGHTERS? WHAT HAS HAPPENED TO OUR COUNTRY?

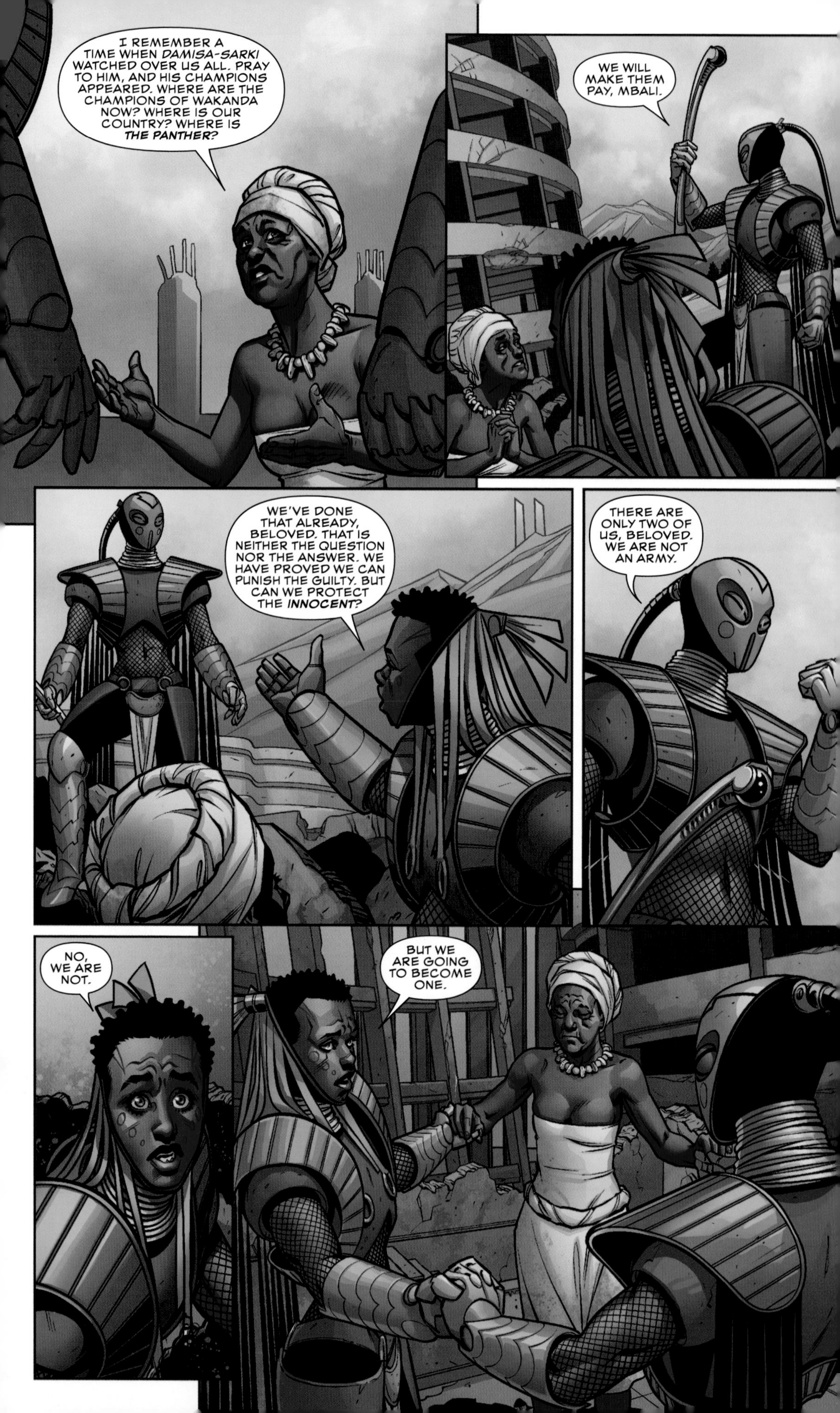
I REMEMBER A TIME WHEN DAMISA-SARKI WATCHED OVER US ALL. PRAY TO HIM, AND HIS CHAMPIONS APPEARED. WHERE ARE THE CHAMPIONS OF WAKANDA NOW? WHERE IS OUR COUNTRY? WHERE IS THE PANTHER?
WE WILL MAKE THEM PAY, MBALI.
WE'VE DONE THAT ALREADY, BELOVED. THAT IS NEITHER THE QUESTION NOR THE ANSWER. WE HAVE PROVED WE CAN PUNISH THE GUILTY. BUT CAN WE PROTECT THE INNOCENT?
THERE ARE ONLY TWO OF US, BELOVED. WE ARE NOT AN ARMY.
NO, WE ARE NOT.
BUT WE ARE GOING TO BECOME ONE.

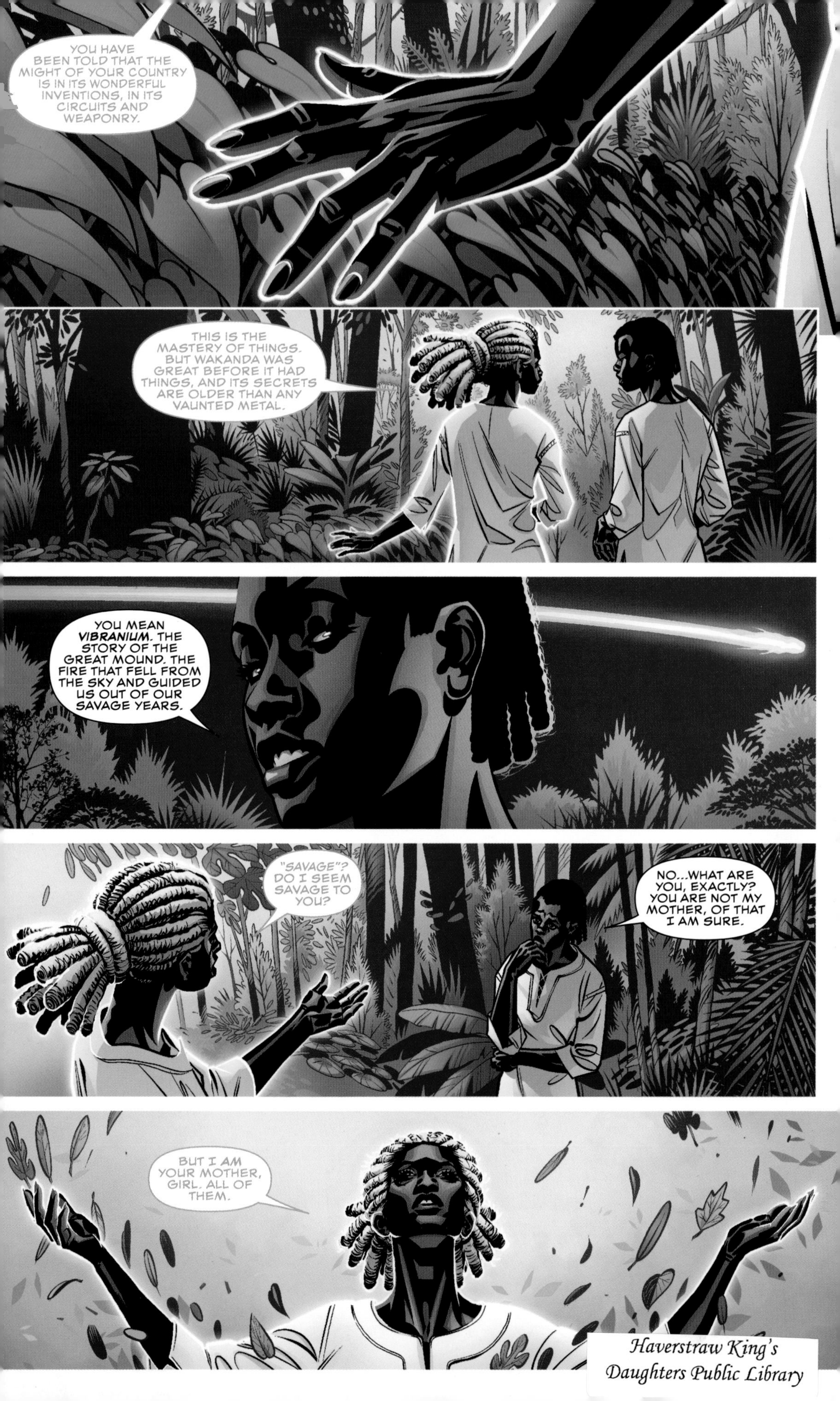
YOU HAVE BEEN TOLD THAT THE MIGHT OF YOUR COUNTRY IS IN ITS WONDERFUL INVENTIONS, IN ITS CIRCUITS AND WEAPONRY.
THIS IS THE MASTERY OF THINGS. BUT WAKANDA WAS GREAT BEFORE IT HAD THINGS, AND ITS SECRETS ARE OLDER THAN ANY VAUNTED METAL.
YOU MEAN *VIBRANIUM*. THE STORY OF THE GREAT MOUND. THE FIRE THAT FELL FROM THE SKY AND GUIDED US OUT OF OUR SAVAGE YEARS.
"*SAVAGE*"? DO I SEEM SAVAGE TO YOU?
NO...WHAT ARE YOU, EXACTLY? YOU ARE NOT MY MOTHER, OF THAT I AM SURE.
BUT I *AM* YOUR MOTHER, GIRL. ALL OF THEM.

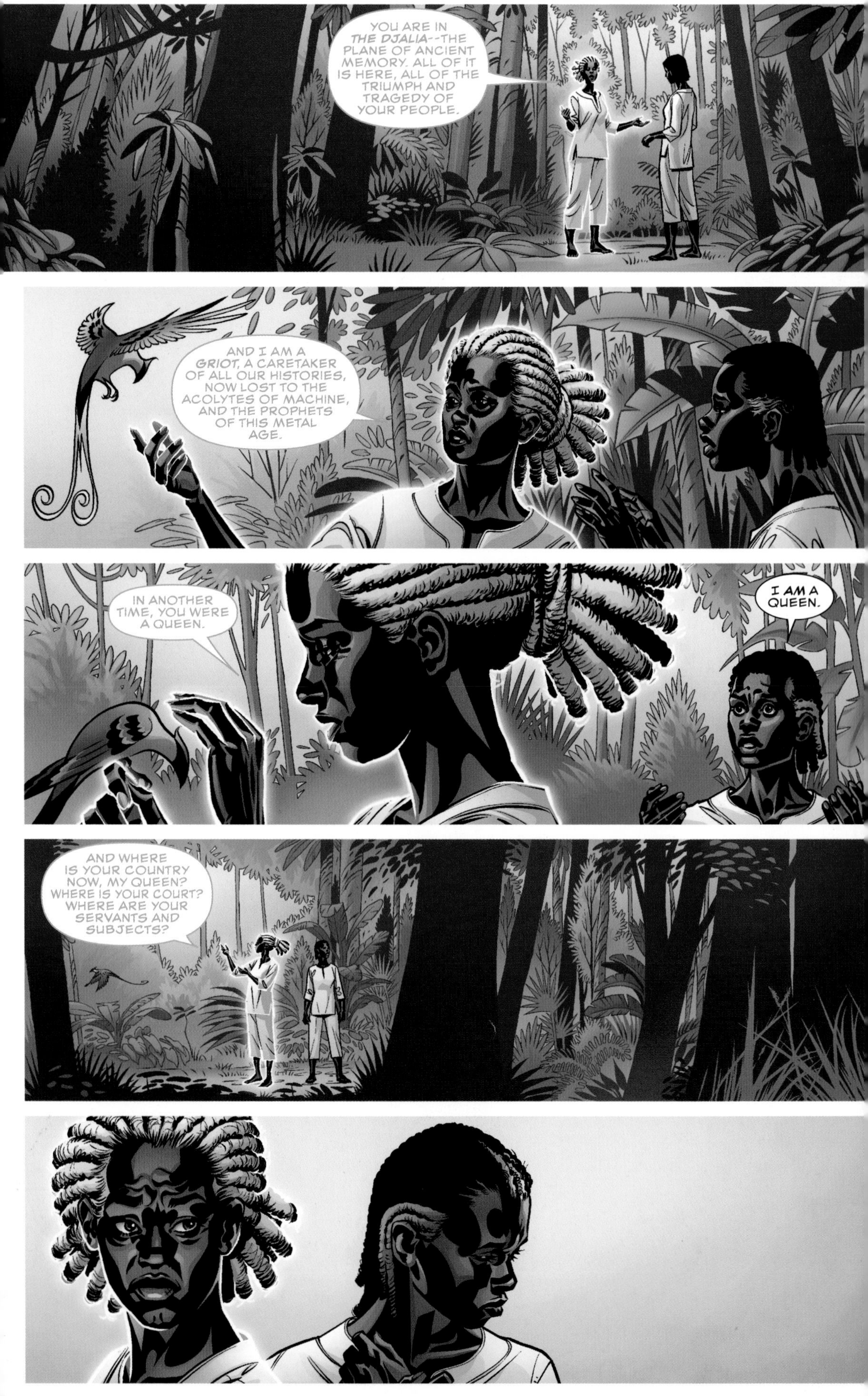
YOU ARE IN THE DJALIA--THE PLANE OF ANCIENT MEMORY. ALL OF IT IS HERE, ALL OF THE TRIUMPH AND TRAGEDY OF YOUR PEOPLE.
AND I AM A GRIOT, A CARETAKER OF ALL OUR HISTORIES, NOW LOST TO THE ACOLYTES OF MACHINE, AND THE PROPHETS OF THIS METAL AGE.
IN ANOTHER TIME, YOU WERE A QUEEN.
I AM A QUEEN.
AND WHERE IS YOUR COUNTRY NOW, MY QUEEN? WHERE IS YOUR COURT? WHERE ARE YOUR SERVANTS AND SUBJECTS?

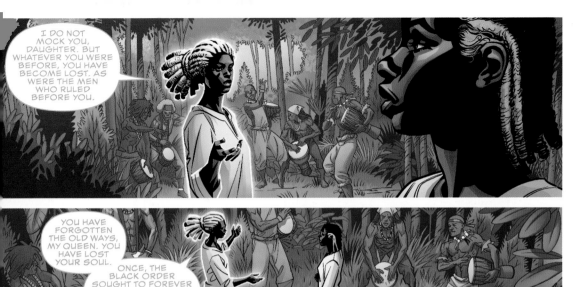

I DO NOT MOCK YOU, DAUGHTER. BUT WHATEVER YOU WERE BEFORE, YOU HAVE BECOME LOST. AS WERE THE MEN WHO RULED BEFORE YOU.

YOU HAVE FORGOTTEN THE OLD WAYS, MY QUEEN. YOU HAVE LOST YOUR SOUL.

ONCE, THE BLACK ORDER SOUGHT TO FOREVER BANISH YOU. BUT THEY KNEW NOT YOUR DESTINATION. THEY KNEW NOTHING OF THE DJALIA.

HERE WE WILL ARM YOU, NOT WITH THE SPEAR, BUT WITH THE DRUM, FOR IT IS THE DRUM THAT CARRIES THE GREATEST POWER OF ALL...

AND WHAT... WHAT IS THAT, MOTHER?

THE POWER OF MEMORY, DAUGHTER. THE POWER OF OUR SONG.

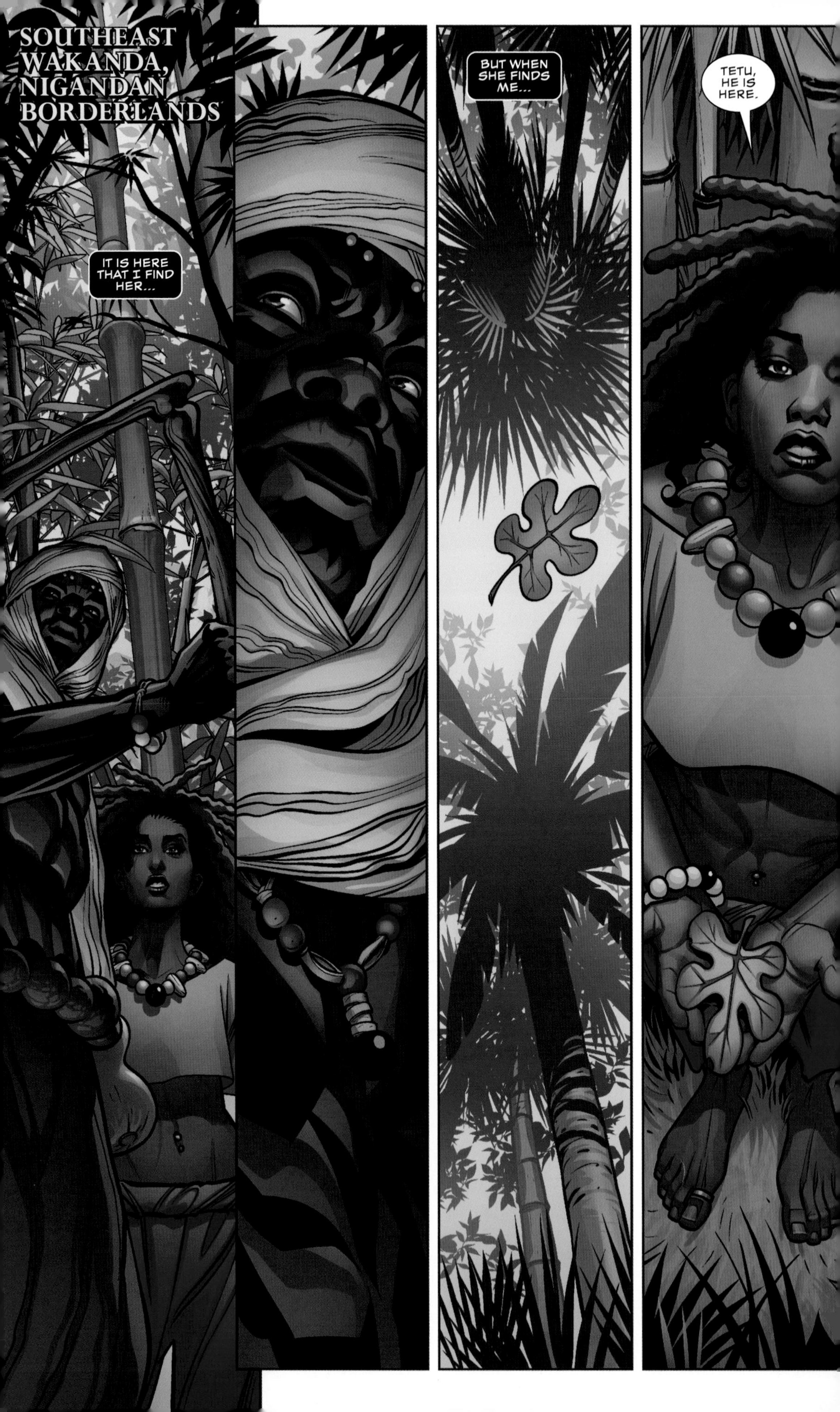
SOUTHEAST WAKANDA, NIGANDAN BORDERLANDS
IT IS HERE THAT I FIND HER...
BUT WHEN SHE FINDS ME...
TETU, HE IS HERE.

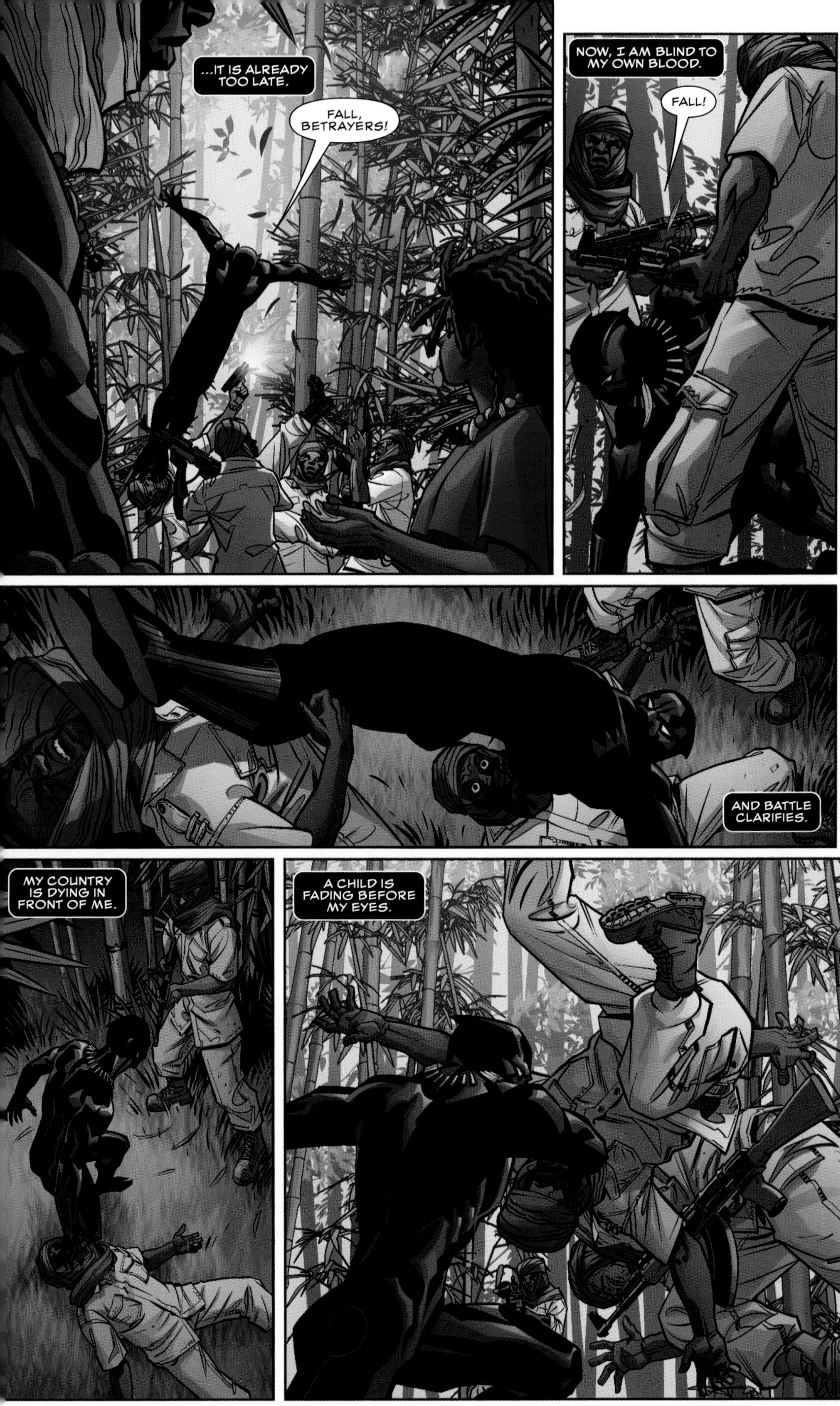
...IT IS ALREADY TOO LATE.
FALL, BETRAYERS!
NOW, I AM BLIND TO MY OWN BLOOD.
FALL!
AND BATTLE CLARIFIES.
MY COUNTRY IS DYING IN FRONT OF ME.
A CHILD IS FADING BEFORE MY EYES.

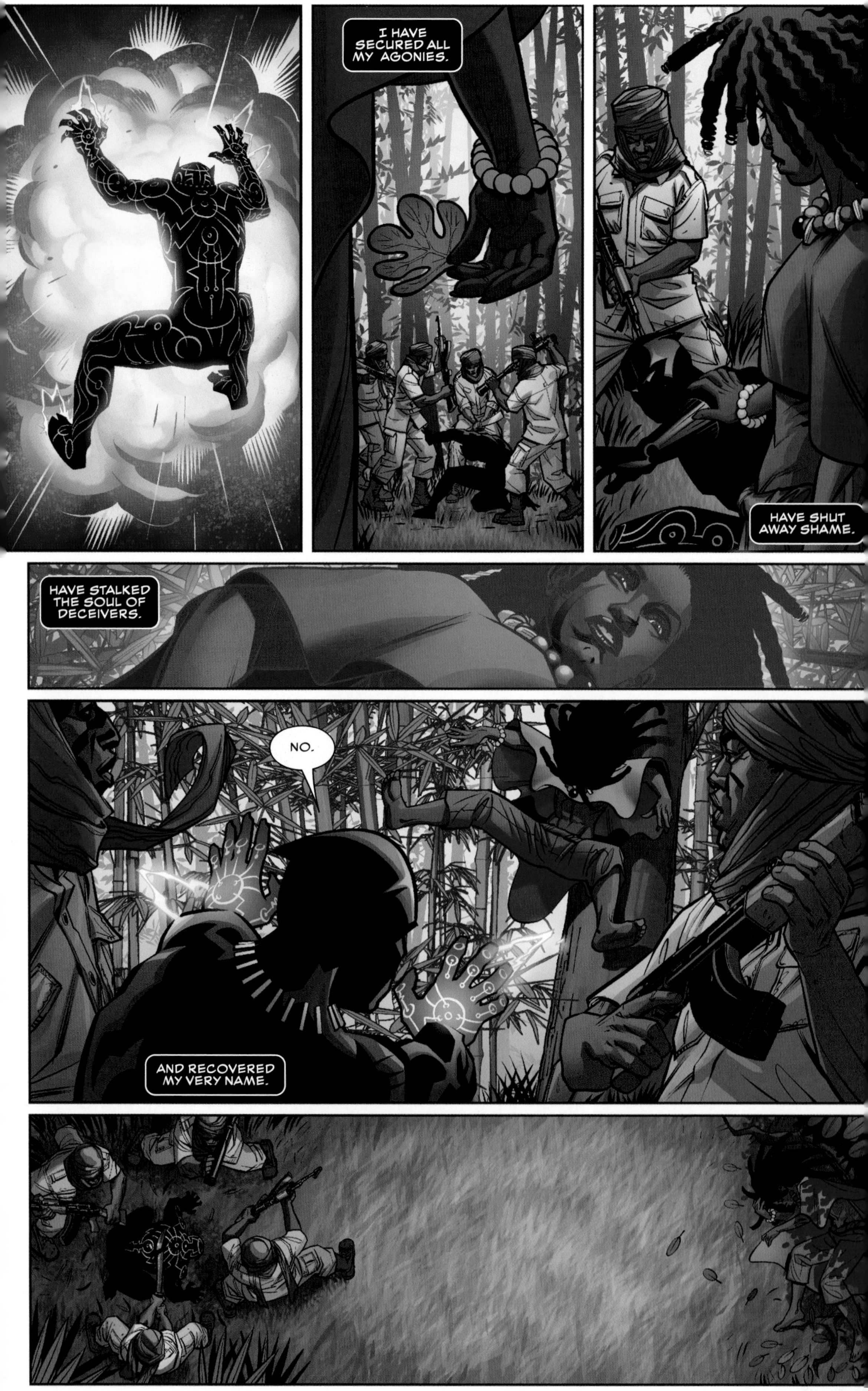
I HAVE SECURED ALL MY AGONIES.
HAVE SHUT AWAY SHAME.
HAVE STALKED THE SOUL OF DECEIVERS.
NO.
AND RECOVERED MY VERY NAME.

NOW, WAR DOGS!

WE ARE WITH YOU, MY KING!

BUT CALAMITY SURROUNDS US.

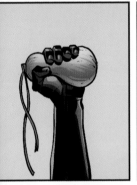

AND I AM WITH YOU, TOO.

THE PAST OVERWHELMS US.

YOU DARE ACCUSE US OF TREACHERY...

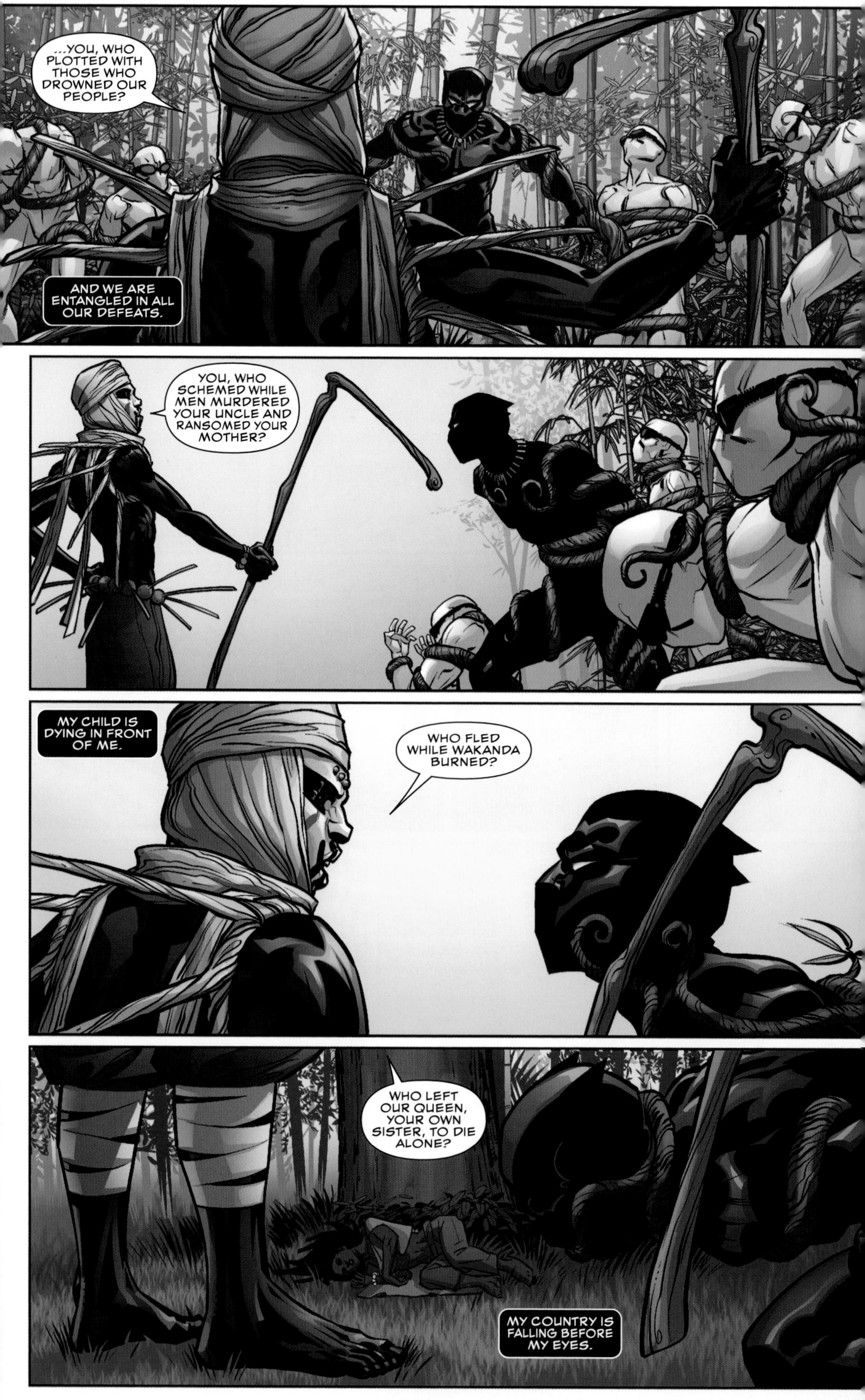
...YOU, WHO PLOTTED WITH THOSE WHO DROWNED OUR PEOPLE?
AND WE ARE ENTANGLED IN ALL OUR DEFEATS.
YOU, WHO SCHEMED WHILE MEN MURDERED YOUR UNCLE AND RANSOMED YOUR MOTHER?
MY CHILD IS DYING IN FRONT OF ME.
WHO FLED WHILE WAKANDA BURNED?
WHO LEFT OUR QUEEN, YOUR OWN SISTER, TO DIE ALONE?
MY COUNTRY IS FALLING BEFORE MY EYES.

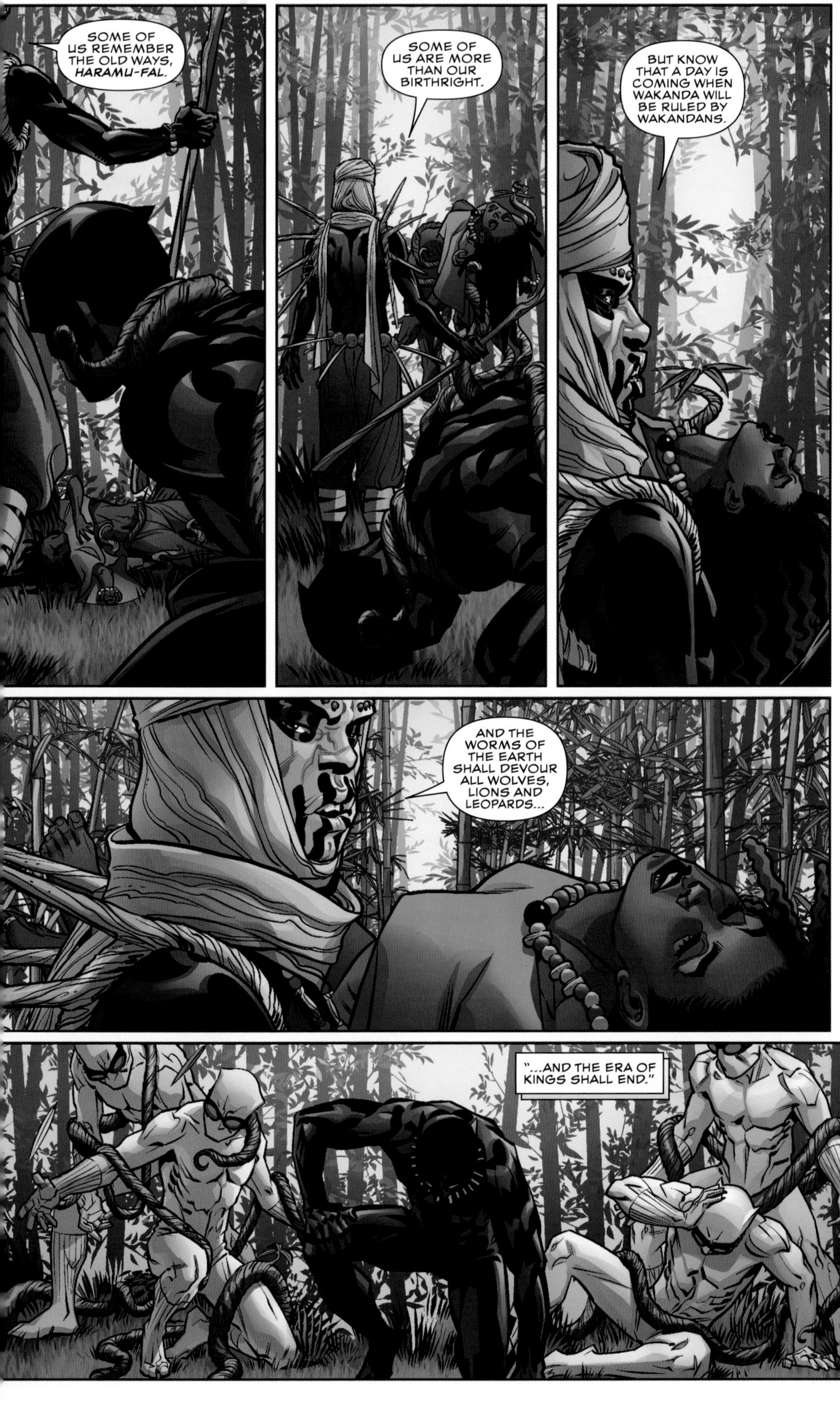
SOME OF US REMEMBER THE OLD WAYS, HARAMU-FAL.
SOME OF US ARE MORE THAN OUR BIRTHRIGHT.
BUT KNOW THAT A DAY IS COMING WHEN WAKANDA WILL BE RULED BY WAKANDANS.
AND THE WORMS OF THE EARTH SHALL DEVOUR ALL WOLVES, LIONS AND LEOPARDS...
"...AND THE ERA OF KINGS SHALL END."

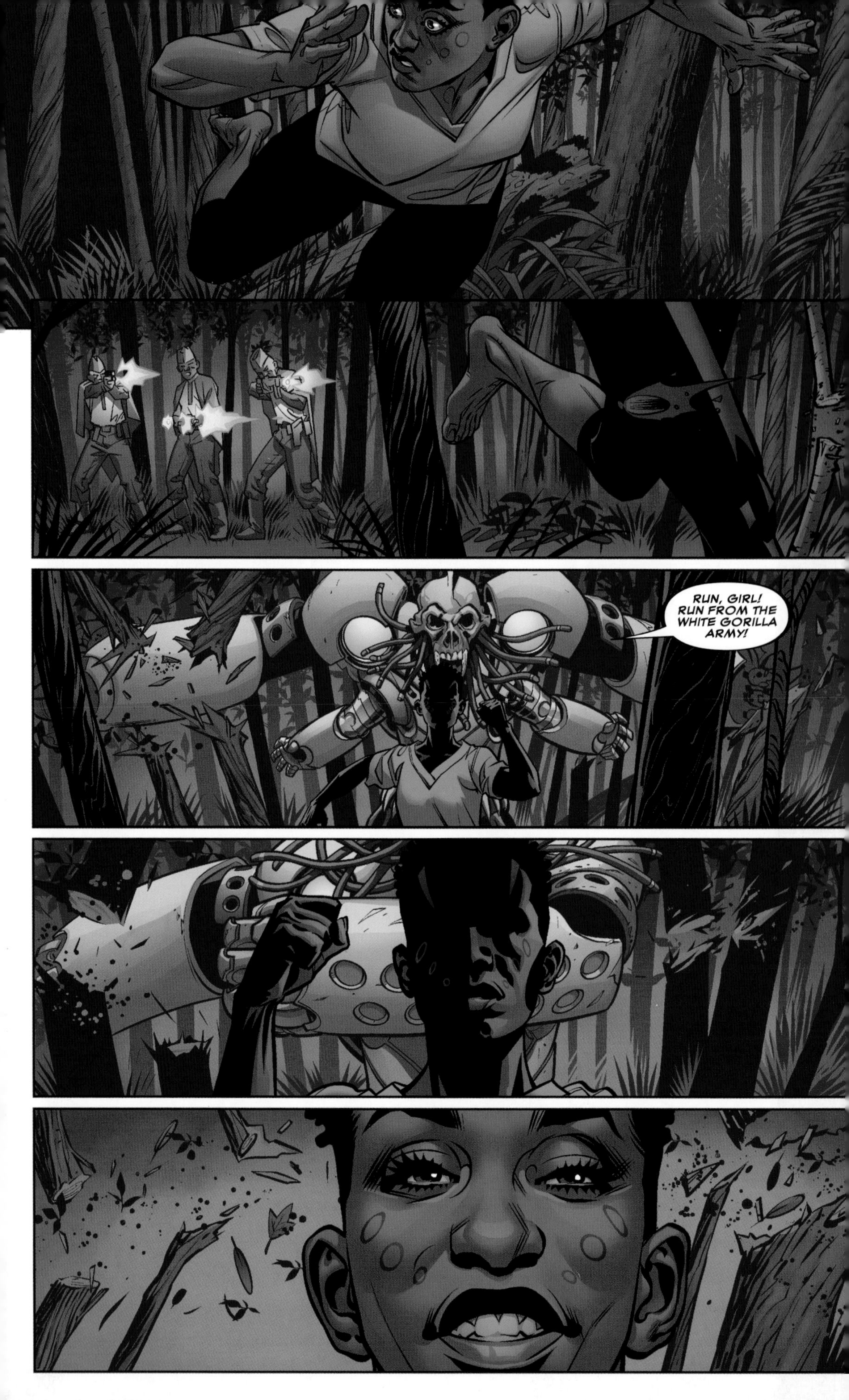
RUN, GIRL! RUN FROM THE WHITE GORILLA ARMY!

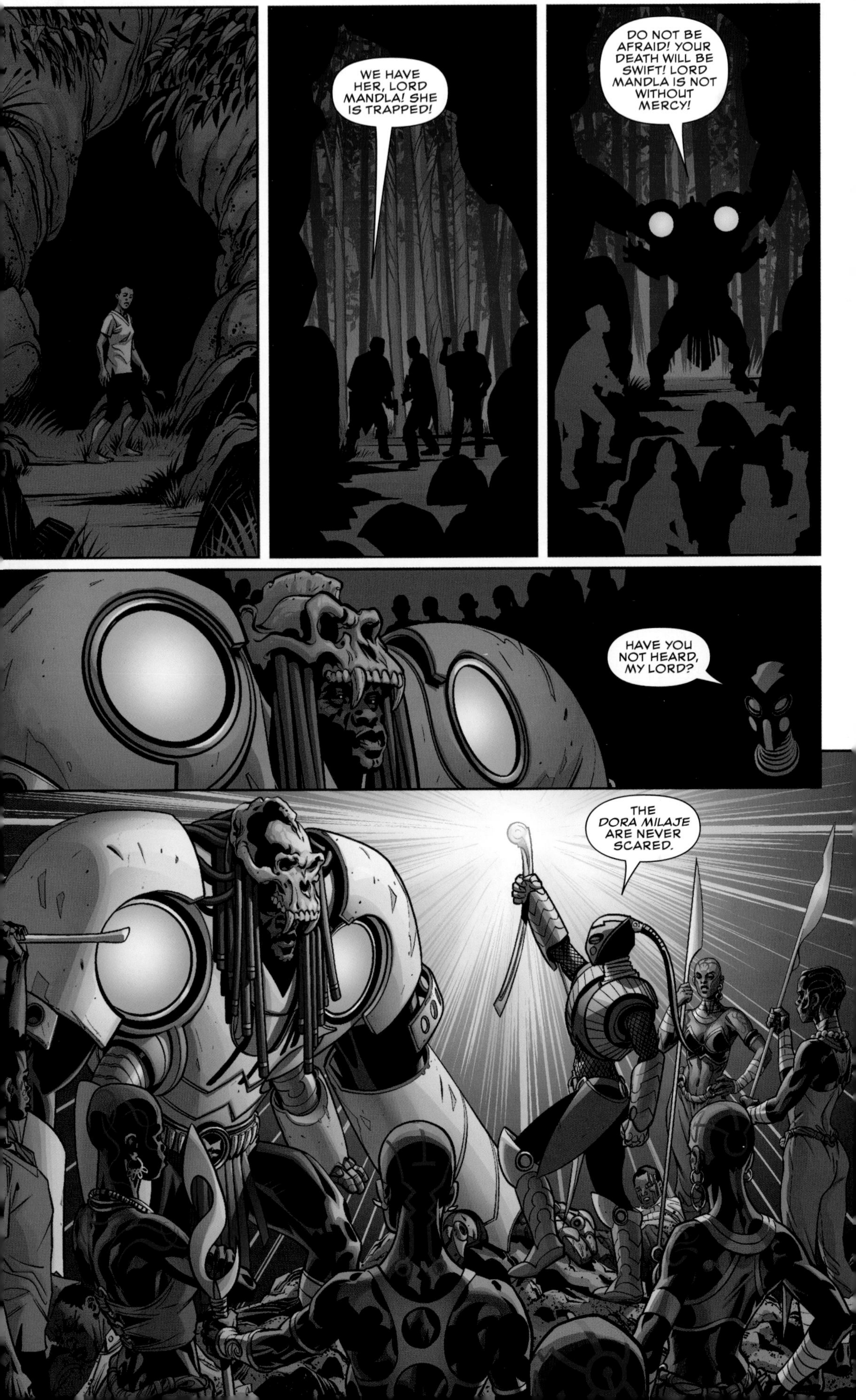
WE HAVE HER, LORD MANDLA! SHE IS TRAPPED!
DO NOT BE AFRAID! YOUR DEATH WILL BE SWIFT! LORD MANDLA IS NOT WITHOUT MERCY!
HAVE YOU NOT HEARD, MY LORD?
THE DORA MILAJE ARE NEVER SCARED.

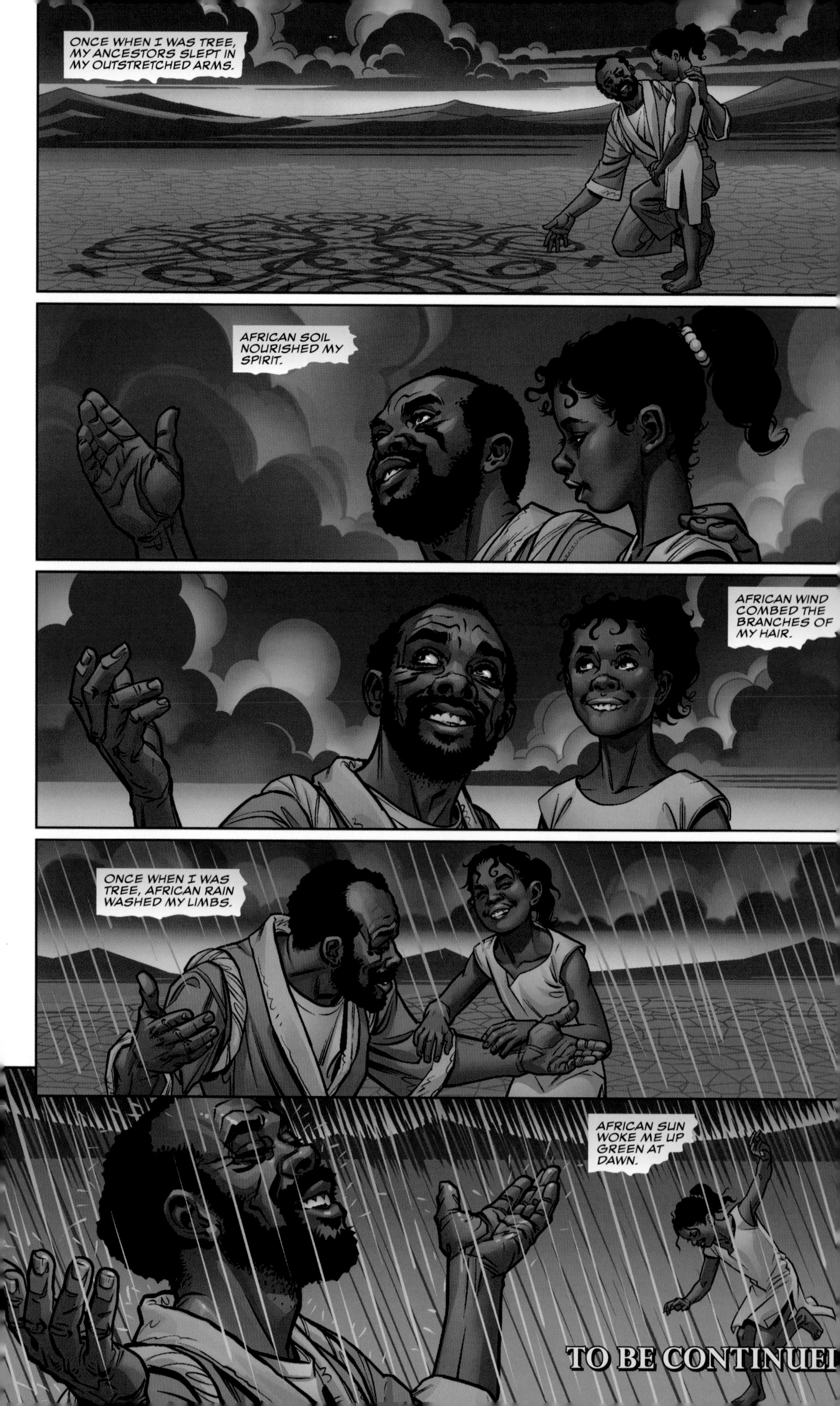

ONCE WHEN I WAS TREE, MY ANCESTORS SLEPT IN MY OUTSTRETCHED ARMS.
AFRICAN SOIL NOURISHED MY SPIRIT.
AFRICAN WIND COMBED THE BRANCHES OF MY HAIR.
ONCE WHEN I WAS TREE, AFRICAN RAIN WASHED MY LIMBS.
AFRICAN SUN WOKE ME UP GREEN AT DAWN.
TO BE CONTINUE